Text copyright © Belinda Hollyer 2001
Illustrations copyright © David Kearney 2001
Book copyright © Wayland 2001

Published in 2001 by Hodder Wayland, an imprint of Hodder Children's Books

This edition published in 2009 by Wayland

The right of Belinda Hollyer to be identified as the
author and David Kearney as the illustrator of this Work
has been asserted by them in accordance with the
Copyright, Designs and Patents Act 1988

A catalogue record for this book is available from
the British Library.

ISBN: 978 0 7502 5752 7

Printed in China

Wayland
338 Euston Road, London NW1 3BH

Wayland is a division of Hachette Children's Books,
an Hachette UK Company
www.hachette.co.uk

Belinda Hollyer has written many books for young people.
To find out more, visit her website and blog at
www.belindahollyer.com

BELIND*

Illustrated by L

WAYLAND

Chapter One

Dad's always liked junk shops. Mum gets cross because he dives off into them when we're out and pokes about for ages when she wants to get on. But I like them, too.

I love the muddle of stuff on the shelves
and tables, and the idea that you might
find something special if you just dig around
a bit. So when we moved to Hewton, Dad
couldn't wait to explore all the likely shops
in the neighbourhood.

And when he found an old photograph
in a funny little back-street shop, I was on
his side about it.

"What do you want *that* for?" asked
Mum.

"It's really interesting," said Dad.
"It's history. Look, Jamie!"

Mum and I peered at the photograph.
It was behind smeary glass inside a filthy old
wooden frame, but when Dad rubbed at the
glass with his sleeve (more frowns from
Mum) you could see a faded group of
people, all dressed in old-fashioned clothes,
standing outside a row of cottages.

The people in the photograph looked stiff and solemn, and a little wary. It seemed like they didn't know what being photographed was all about, and didn't much like it, either. Unfriendly, that was my first thought.

"Turn of the century, I bet!" said Dad proudly. "And I don't mean this last century, either, I mean..." He peered closer. "Hey, wait a minute," he said under his breath. "That's *our* cottage!"

He was right. It *was* Bunhill Cottage, where we'd moved the week before – second from the end of a row of cottages just like now, and looking a lot plainer – but ours for sure. Of course, the cottages had all been done up since then, but you could tell it was the same place. The only difference I could see was that there was no loft conversion window to show where my bedroom is – no sign of that in 1879. (The date was on the back of the frame.)

So we had to have the picture, didn't we? I agreed with Dad, and even Mum gave in without any fuss.

But if I'd known what was going to happen, I'd have chucked the photograph into the far corner of the shop and got us all as far away as I could.

I tell you, it's put me off history for good.

Chapter Two

When we got home, Dad washed the frame
and the glass, polished it all up, put hooks
and string on the back, and hung it in the
front hall. It looked good.

I took a closer look at the people in
the photograph. There were seven of
them, standing right outside our cottage.

There was an old couple who looked as if they might have been grandparents: the old man had a sort of handcart beside him. Then there was a woman who might have been around Mum's age. And then four kids – a toddler hanging on to her sister's skirt with one hand and sucking a bit of rag, and two older boys, as well, around my age. I thought there were too many people to fit in our little place, but Dad said they'd probably all lived together in Bunhill Cottage.

"No money for anywhere bigger, I'd guess," he said. "Low wages, or no wages at all, maybe. They'd have had to cram themselves in and count themselves lucky to have a roof, Jamie."

The kids were barefoot and looked grubby and sad, as though they'd never laughed in their lives. The adults were thin and shabby, too. The whole lot of them looked bad-tempered and mean, and I felt like they were all staring right back at me while I was looking at them. I almost thought one of them shifted slightly – it gave me a shiver.

I dreamed about the kids that night.

In my dream I was asleep in my loft bedroom – which I was, of course, that bit was real – and I woke up surrounded by the children in the photo.

The toddler was sucking her thumb but the others were muttering, too softly for me to hear what they were saying. They were all staring at me, chanting something over and over in a hissing whisper, and taking slow, slow steps towards the bed.

Soon they were all standing over me,
and then the little one reached forward
with her dirty, claw-like little hands, and
touched me—

And I woke up. I was dead frightened,
I can tell you. I couldn't see anything at first
and I thought the kids were still there, before
I came to completely and realized it had
been a dream. There was no sound, and
no sign of anyone.

I switched on the light, to be sure.
No one.

But there was something on the floor.
I got up to see what it was.

A torn rag. Dirty. Damp.

I swear it wasn't mine.

It looked like the rag the little girl had
in the photograph.

Chapter Three

I hardly slept that night, but I woke early anyway. I felt hot and dizzy, and I had a headache. "Probably just not enough sleep," I thought. I didn't want to be sick, with the football season just starting – I had a good chance of being picked for the team at my new school.

As soon as I got dressed I put the rag in my pocket and took it downstairs to have another look at the photo in the hall – not that I *really* thought it was the same rag. I just wanted to check.

But when I looked at the photo again, my stomach lurched and my head started to thump with pain.

I couldn't believe it!

The children had *moved around*. And the girl – the little one who'd been holding the rag – wasn't holding anything at all, now. She was leaning back against her sister's skirt staring straight at me – and holding out her hand! As I stared, my thumping headache somehow turned into a whispery, hissy little voice in my head – and this time I heard what the words were.

"*Mine*," the voice said. "*Mine, give it back!*"

I blinked and shook my head and the voice stopped, but the little kid in the photo still looked straight at me with her hand stretched out, and the others *had* moved since the day before, I just knew it.

Dad came downstairs as I was staring at the photo in horror. I grabbed his arm as he passed.

"Dad, do you remember where the kids were in this?" My voice sounded shaky, and I coughed to cover it up.

"How do you mean, Jamie, where they *were*? Where they are now, I suppose!" laughed Dad.

"No, Dad, seriously. Look!" I pointed.

The day before, the two boys had been in front of the grown-ups, and the girl and the toddler had been on the other side of the group. Now the kids were all standing together at the front, in a bunch. The boys had their fists clenched, too – I was *sure* they hadn't stood like that before.

Dad stared at the photo, and then at me.

"Looks just the same to me," he said cheerfully. Then he started going on about how old the row of cottages was.

I was too worried to listen. Was it me?
Could I have imagined it all?

"...so, would you like to come with me?"
It was Dad. I hadn't heard a word he'd said.

"Wakey, wakey! I said, would you like to
come to the local library with me and ask
about Bunhill Cottage?" he said patiently.

I agreed. If I could find out more about
the people in the photograph, it might help
me work out what was going on.

Chapter Four

Dad met me after school and we got a bus to the library. The reference librarian and Dad started going on at each other about our row of cottages like it was a subject on a quiz show, and I tuned out, thinking about the photo again. But I pricked up my ears when the librarian said something about a mysterious death. Well, wouldn't you?

Apparently, there was a local story about a family who'd lived in the cottages – the librarian didn't know which one, but a lurch in the pit of my stomach told me that I knew, all right.

"The father worked in the mill. That whole row was mill cottages, you know. You had to work at the mill to rent one. The kids were probably mill workers, too. Times were hard back then for everyone," said the librarian. "But then the father lost his arm in an accident at the mill, so he couldn't work there any more. Next thing, the family's evicted from their home. No rights, no workers' compensation then – the whole lot of them had to leave, with no money and no place to go."

I had a funny feeling it was going to
get worse. It did.

The librarian continued. "Story is, the
father went off searching for other work –
and never came back. Died in a storm on
the moors, people said. The kids ended up
in the poorhouse. It's all in our local
resource section documents, mill history
and all, if you'd like to look."

By this time I'd really freaked out, so
when Dad said he'd come back another
day, I was relieved.

As soon as we were on the bus again
I tried to tell Dad about my dream, and
about the photograph changing. I explained
as best I could but I could see he thought
I was over-reacting.

"Oh, Jamie! There goes that imagination
of yours again," he said. "You must have
dreamed it."

I wished that was true. I hoped it was
true. I almost believed it was, until I put
my hand in my pocket and felt the old rag.
But I didn't say any more. What did an old
rag prove?

I only looked
sideways at the
photo that
afternoon. At least
it looked as though
everyone was in
the same place as
they had been that
morning.

And I didn't
mean to check
again on my way
up to bed. I'd had
enough of moving
photos and horrible stories and stuff. I
didn't care, I told myself, if they were all
standing on their heads.

But I did just glance as I walked past.
And as I did, the kids moved again. I saw
the flicker out of the corner of my eye.

I felt sick, but I stopped, and made
myself look properly.

The kids... now the kids were standing
over at the side *with someone else*. A tall, thin
man who hadn't been there before...

I blinked and then opened my eyes again.

No new man. He'd gone. The kids were at
the front again, staring back at me.

Chapter Five

It took me ages to get off to sleep that night,
but I dropped off in the end. I know that,
because the kids woke me up again in
the middle of the night. This time I knew
I wasn't dreaming. I just wasn't sure that I
was in my own room. Wherever I was, it was
pitch dark. My loft room always got a bit of
streetlight through the window. And my
room smelled, well, normal. This didn't:
there was a sour, musty smell in the air.

I knew I wasn't alone, either. I'd heard a noise – it had woken me up. What was it? And then it came again, a soft scratching, right beside me. I sat up, banged my head on something, and yelped with pain.

"Sssh," whispered someone, right beside me. Then I heard the scratching noise again, and this time a light flared.

The three older kids from the photo were crouching beside me, and one of the boys was holding a flickering candle.

And we were all in – well, it *wasn't* my bedroom, but it did look familiar... I glanced around, trying to keep one eye on the kids at the same time. And I realized it *was* the loft of our house, before it was turned into my bedroom. No walls or ceiling, just the rough outside walls and roof beams crossing the space – that's what I'd bumped my head on.

The kids stared at me, the candlelight flickering across their faces. I stared back, trying not to panic. (Well, wouldn't *you* feel like panicking? If you found yourself stuck in a smelly loft a hundred years back in time, with a group of kids who can only be ghosts and who look like they hate you?)

"Our Sis wants her rag back," said the boy holding the candle.

"Give it us," they all chanted together, their eyes glittering.

"This is our room and we want our Da." That was the girl hissing at me again.

"Find him," they all chanted together.

I stared at them in disbelief.

"Look," I said cautiously. "I'll give you back the rag, only it's not here. It's in my jeans' pocket, in *my* room. But I don't know how to find your dad."

The kids shifted around a bit, but they didn't say anything. Then the girl moved closer, peering at me, almost touching me. I tried not to flinch away.

"The *pho-to-graph*," she said carefully, like it was a foreign word.

"But he's not in it," I said. "Your dad isn't there. Unless – was that him I saw tonight? Just for a moment?" I was starting to babble a bit now but I didn't take my eyes off her, which is how I saw that her eyes suddenly filled with tears. I didn't know ghosts could cry.

"We remember him," she said softly. "If we all remember together we can get him back again, but—"

"He can't stay." That was one of the boys.

"Put him back. Back to stay," said the girl.

Yeah, I know, but that's what she said. *Put him back.*

And while I was gaping at her, the kids just sort of faded away. *Creepy.* And then I was back in my own bed and the light was showing through the blinds, and I could tell it was morning.

Chapter Six

The rag... Put back their father...

I ask you. But I had to start somewhere, if I wanted them to stop haunting me.

So I got the rag out of my jeans, took it downstairs, and held it up in front of the photo in the hall.

"There you are, Sis," I said. "For you."

I left the rag in my room that night. I tried to stay awake to see if the kids would come and get it. Not that I wanted to see them again – I just wanted proof it was really happening and not just my imagination.

But it didn't work out as easily as that. I drifted off to sleep anyway, and the rag had vanished by morning.

The bit about their dad was a whole lot harder. I didn't know why they'd chosen me to help, and to be honest I almost gave up. The kids left me alone for nearly a week, too, but just when I began to think it was over, they were back again.

They all stood around my bed and stared at me. Didn't say a word, didn't whisper or chant or hiss. Just stared, eyes glittering in the candlelit dark, bodies fading in and out of the shadows. Stayed for hours. It was awful. It was the memory of those glittering eyes that kept me trying to work out what to do.

As I saw it, there were only a few things I could try. I started thinking about *really* finding their Dad, looking on the moor for his body, but I gave that up fast. (No clues about where to look, and way too gruesome.) Maybe I could paint a picture of him, I thought. Try to remember what he looked like, paint him and hang that up in the hall. But not even my best friend would say I was good at art, and I knew it would have to be good to work.

Then I thought about putting him back in the photo. I knew you could do that on computers – mess around with photos, add stuff to them – but I didn't know how. And I didn't have a photo of him to add.

It was another week before I finally worked it out. I was in bed but not sleeping, frightened that the kids would come back and stare at me all night again, when I remembered what the librarian had said.

There was stuff about the mill in their resource section.

If there was a photo of Bunhill Cottage, maybe there were others, too. And just maybe...

It was worth a try.

When I asked the librarian about photos of the mill workers I struck gold! There was a whole box file of them, and I finally found one that had a group of adults and kids standing in front of a loom.

The kids caught my eye first – I
recognized the older boy and girl from our
photo. And they were standing beside a tall,
thin, serious-looking man. He had his hands
on their shoulders.

It had to be him!

I told Dad what I'd found. It wasn't hard to talk him into buying a print of the photo and hanging it next to the other one. And he loved all the history, he even found out the family's name, and renamed the cottage after them. I thought the kids would like that.

Sometimes I think I see the thin man in the cottage photograph again – but when I look properly, he's not there. The kids have returned to their original positions, though, and I've had no more bad dreams or visits in the night. But I still check on them every time I go through the hall, just in case.

The thing is, if they want anything else, they know where to find me.

DARE TO BE SCARED!

Are you brave enough to try more titles in the Tremors series? They're guaranteed to chill your spine...

Play... if you dare by Ruth Symes
Rosie can hardly believe her luck when she finds the computer game at a car boot sale. "Play... if you dare," the game challenges. So she does. Further and further she plays, each level of the game scarier than the last. Then she reaches the last level. "Play... if you dare," repeats the game. But if she does, she could be trapped for ever...

The Claygate Hound by Jan Dean
On the school camp to Claygate, Billy is determined to scare everyone with his terrifying stories of the Claygate Hound, a vicious ghost dog said to lurk nearby. Ryan and Zeb ignore his warnings and explore the woods. They hear a ghostly howl – and run. Has Billy been speaking the truth, or is there a more terrifying reason for what they have heard?

The Empty Grave by Rebecca Lisle
When Jay visits her cousin at Gulliver House, strange things start to happen. Who is the mysterious child that cries in the night? And what is behind the sealed door? Jay and Freddie must discover the truth before it's too late...

All these books and many more can be purchased from your local bookseller. For more information about Tremors, write to: The Sales Department, Hachette Children's Books, 338 Euston Road, London NW1 3BH.